Dear Princess Kooki,

I sit behind you on the school shuttle, and I think you have lovely hair and you smell like flipberry fizz-dips...

I plan to rule the universe and I'd like you to be my queen. I promise to be nice to your mum and dad when I'm King of Space.

Lots of love,

Rex xxx

D0418820

To Mumbot, who
fed me custard while
I came up with a plan...
love from
your Doodlebot x

A TEMPLAR BOOK

First published in the UK in 2013
by Templar Publishing,
an imprint of The Templar Company Limited,
Deepdene Lodge, Deepdene Avenue,
Dorking, Surrey, RH5 4AT, UK
www.templarco.co.uk

Copyright © 2013 by Jonny Duddle

First edition

All rights reserved

ISBN 978-1-84877-226-7

Edited by Libby Hamilton

Printed in China

THE KING OF SPACE

by Jonny Duddle

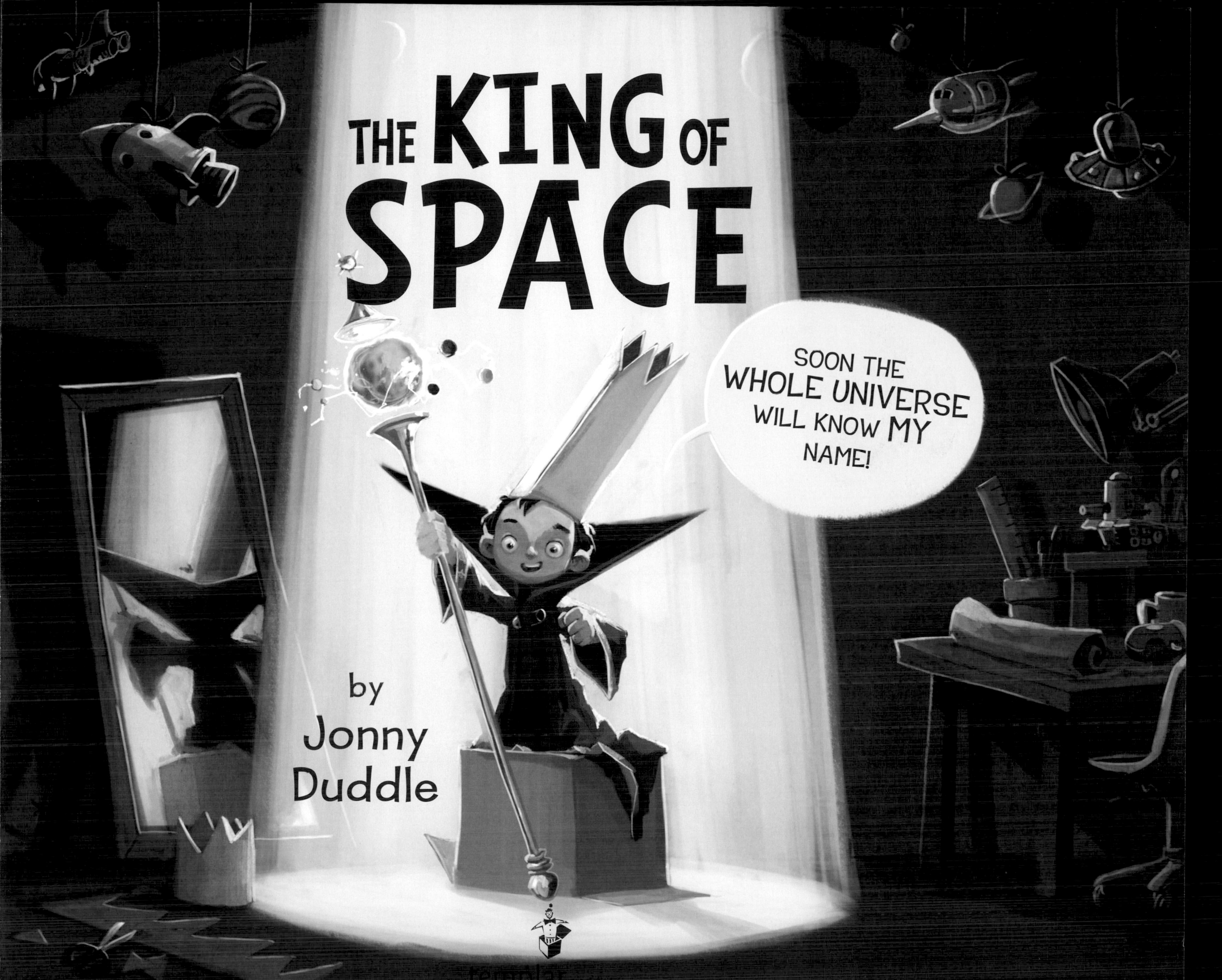

Mum and Dad say I have too much energy, so they have to keep me busy.

But on this particular night, I was too busy to clean my room.

I'd just thought up my BIGGEST and BESTEST PLAN EVER!

Annoyingly, I couldn't get going straight away
because the next day I had to go
to Mini Galactic Citizen School.

TODAY, SPROGLETS,
I'D LIKE EACH OF YOU
TO TELL THE CLASS
WHAT YOU WANT TO BE
WHEN YOU GROW UP.

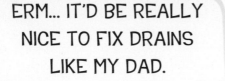

I'M GOING TO FLY SPACE FREIGHTERS. VROOOOOM!

ERM... IT'D BE REALLY NICE TO FIX DRAINS LIKE MY DAD.

I JUST WANNA MAKE COMPUTER GAMES, DUDE!

YES, MA'AM. I'M TRAINING TO BE A SPACE MARINE, MA'AM!

WELL, MISS BRAIN...

I'VE DEVELOPED A CLEVER PLAN.

A PLAN TO TAKE ME FROM THIS LOWLY CLASSROOM TO THE FURTHEST REACHES OF SPACE!

I WILL CREATE AN ARMY SO POWERFUL THAT ONLY THE MOST FOOLISH WILL DARE STAND AGAINST ME!

I WILL CRUSH PLANETS AND SQUISH SOLAR SYSTEMS!

SOON THE WHOLE UNIVERSE WILL KNOW MY NAME...

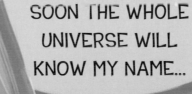

I WILL BE THE KING OF SPACE!

For homework that night, Miss Brain asked us to each build a robot that could do something helpful.

I'M GOING TO BUILD THE **BEST** ROBOT!

AND IT WON'T DO **BORING** HELPFUL STUFF.

MY ROBOT WILL **CRUSH** ALL OTHER ROBOTS!

I WILL CALL IT MY **WARBOT!**

Miss Brain said she was very impressed with everybody else's robots...

Blip's spaceship-washbot...

Xarg's toast-o-matic (with net)...

Zorick's lawnmower-machine...

and even Glob's drain-unblocking-droid.

But I don't think
she was too keen
on my WARBOT!

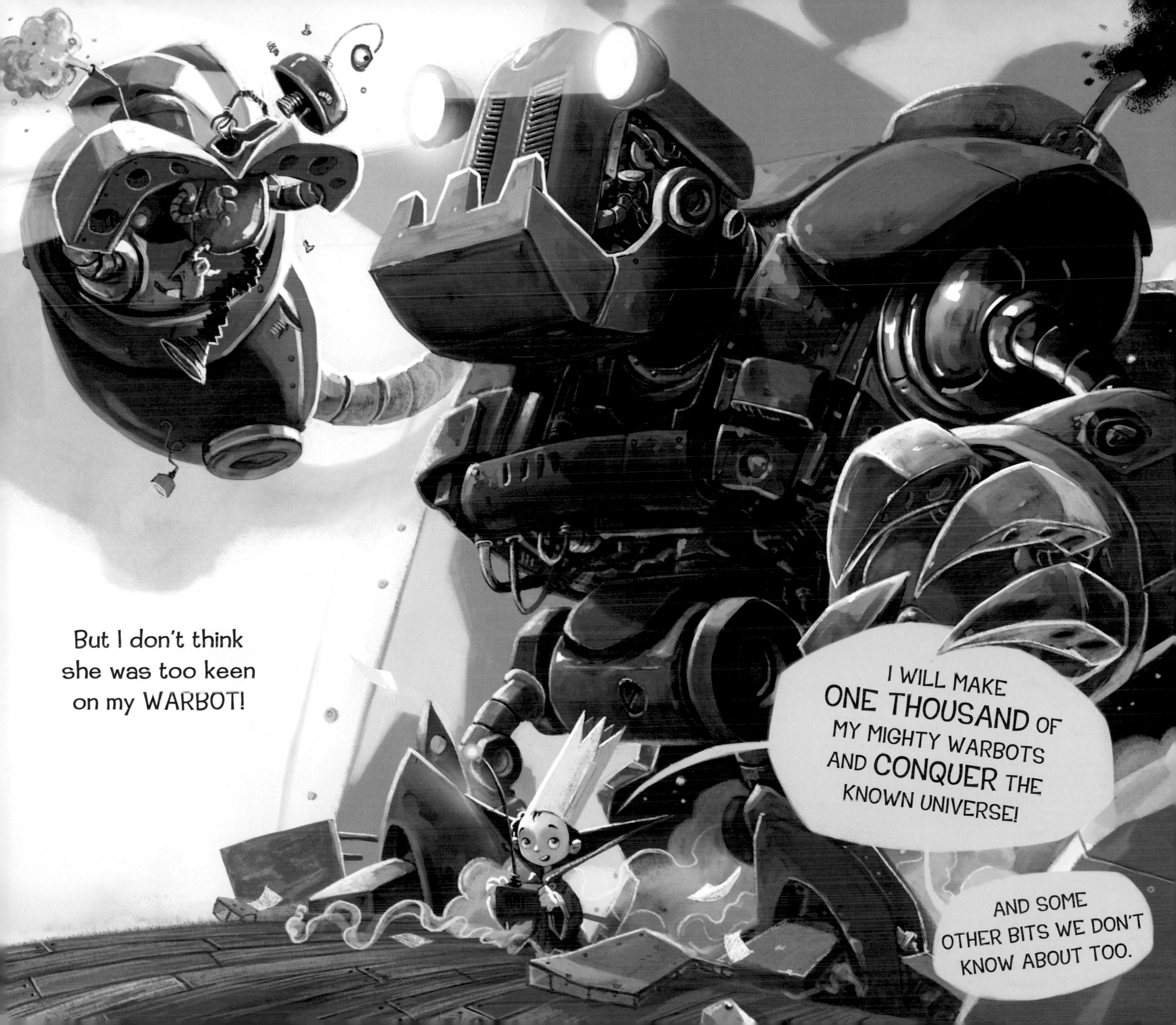

Miss Brain asked my mum and dad to come into school.

At playtime, Miss Brain made me stay inside to type "School is more important than being the King of Space" one hundred times.

WHAT DOES SHE KNOW?

I WILL be the King of Space!
I WILL be the King of Space!
I WILL be the King of Space!
I WILL be the King of Space!
I WILL be the King of Sp_

NOTHING IS MORE IMPORTANT THAN BEING THE KING OF SPACE!

After school,
my warbot used its
digger attachment
to hollow out my
secret headquarters.

In exchange for an
astro-cookie and
two bottles of fizz-dip,
my very clever friend
Blip helped me to build
my WARBOT FACTORY!

Blip said he wouldn't tell anyone about it, as long as I promised to only make nice, friendly robots.

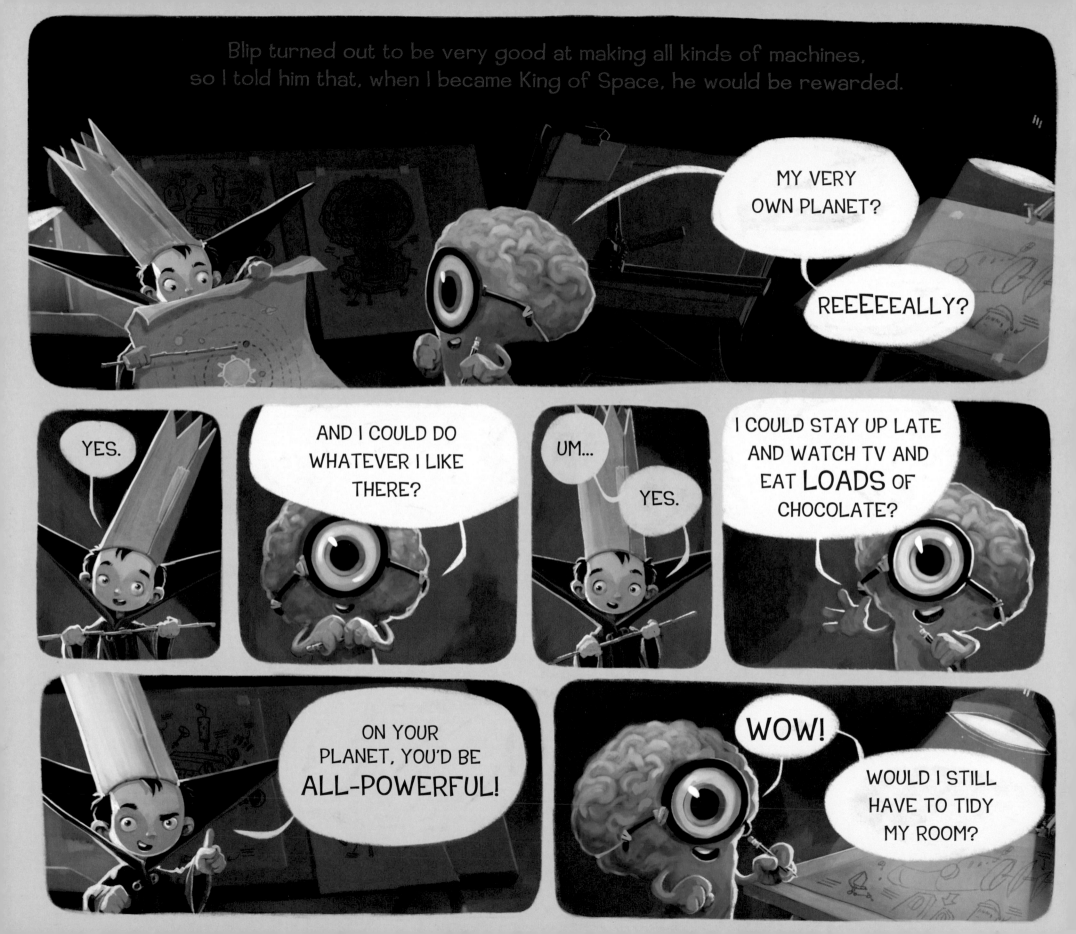

He might not have quite got the idea, but Blip did fit dung-blasters to all my warbots and build my Dastardly Dung Ray before he went home for his dinner.

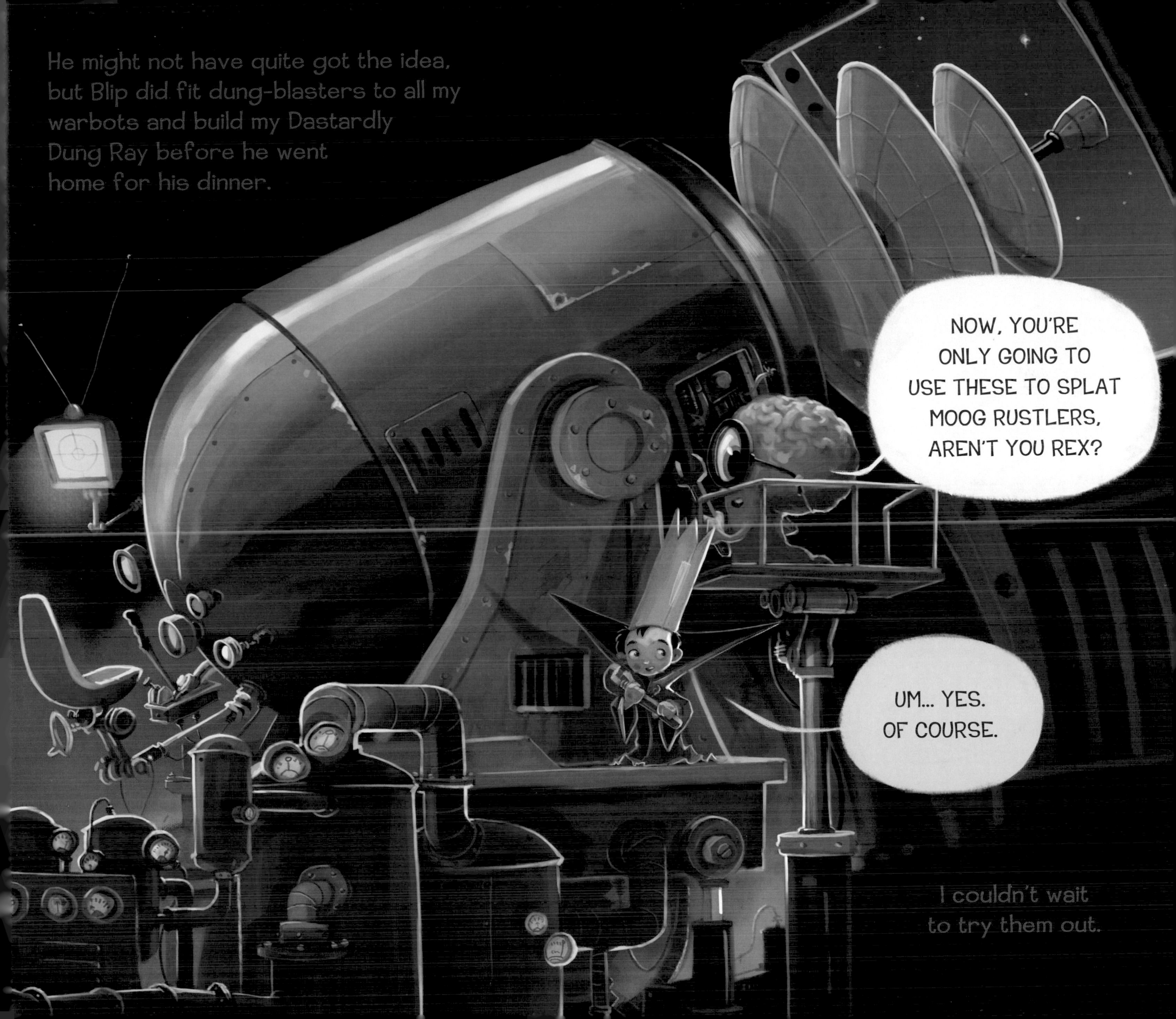

I couldn't wait to try them out.

That weekend, while Mum thought I was at a sleepover at Xarg's house, I crushed all resistance in the Western Spiral.

Mum did say that I looked a bit tired
when she picked me up in the morning.

It turned out that, while I'd been away, my worker droids had finished building my throne room.

So I decided it was time for my CORONATION!

I handed out some invitations at school, making everyone promise that they wouldn't tell their mums and dads.

Blip made a clever machine that could transmit live TV images,
so everyone in the universe had to watch my coronation ceremony
whether they liked it or not.

REX

I NOW
CROWN MYSELF
THE **KING** OF
SPACE!

CLAP
NOW!

I gave a
party bag
to everyone
who clapped a lot.

Just to be on the safe side, I kidnapped Emperor Bob's daughter, Princess Kooki.

After that, Princess Kooki gave me the silent treatment.

I tried to sneak past Mum and Dad to get the choco-goo.
There was lots of great stuff on the news about my warbots taking over
the universe and Princess Kooki being held hostage.

But when I went outside, something wasn't right...

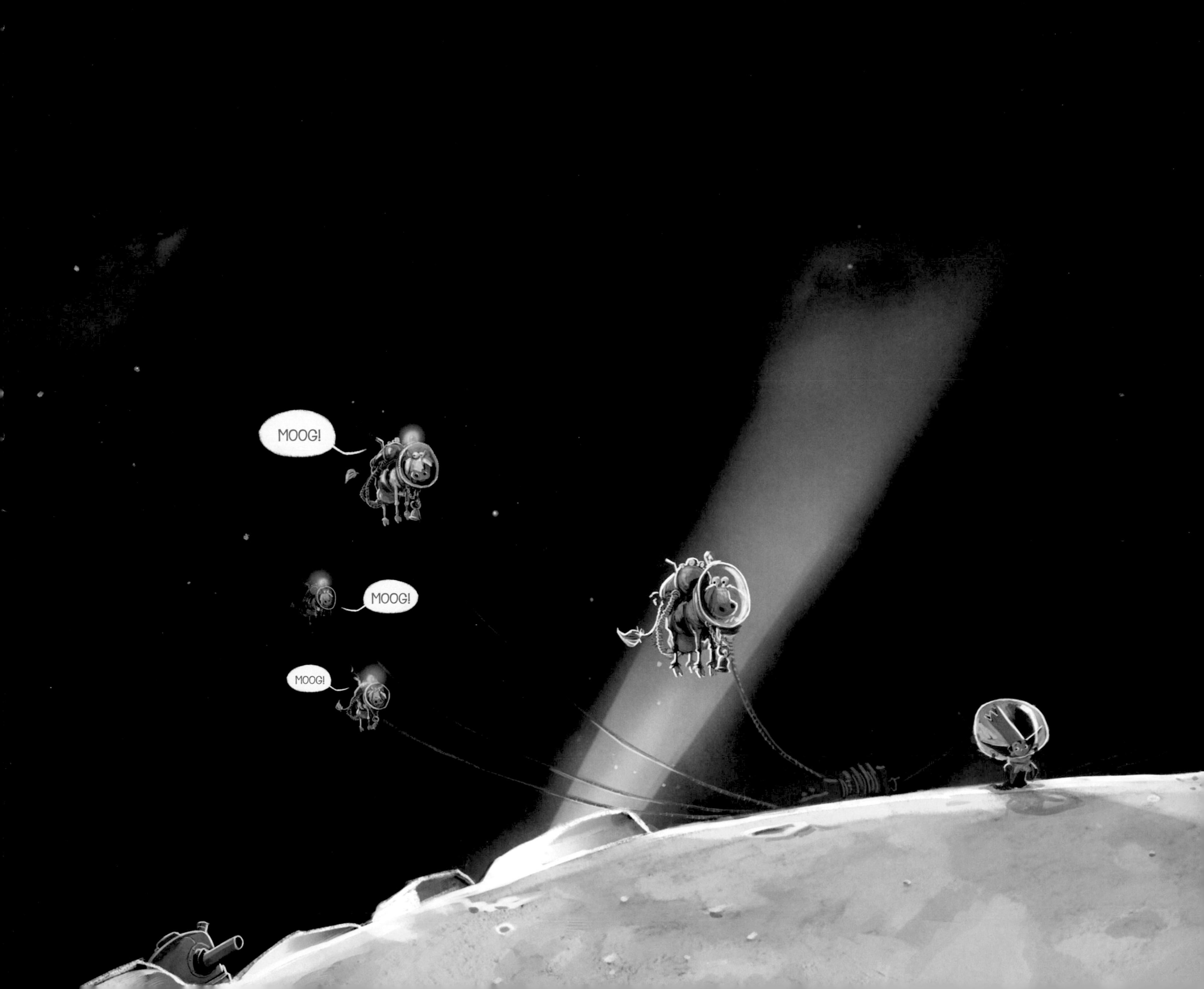

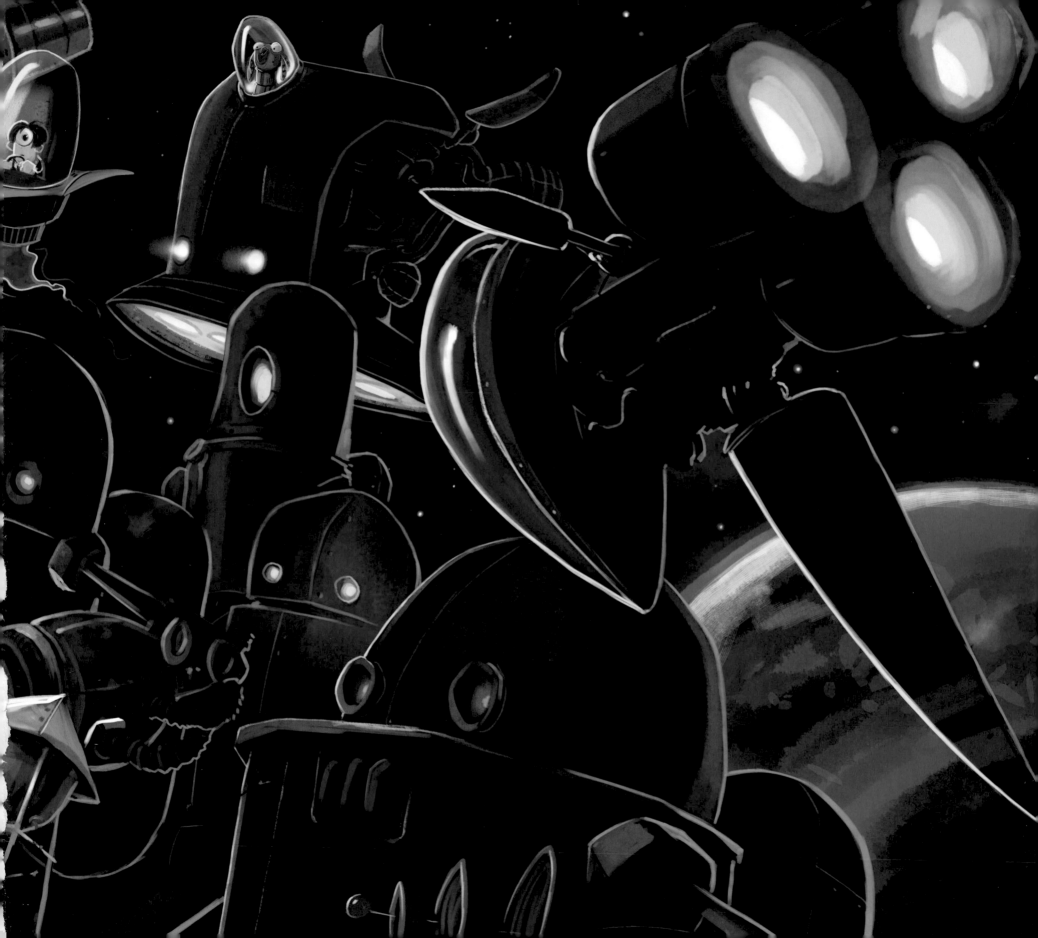

Mum said she was going outside to have a word with the Galactic Alliance.

NOW, YOU LISTEN HERE! REX IS A VERY TIRED LITTLE BOY. HE DOESN'T WANT TO PLAY ANYMORE, SO I THINK IT'S TIME YOU **ALL** WENT HOME!

OH, AND PRINCESS KOOKI SAYS SHE **DOESN'T** WANT TO STAY FOR CHOCO-GOO, SO COULD YOUR MAJESTY POP DOWN AND TAKE HER BACK WITH YOU?

Luckily, even the Galactic Alliance can't say no to Mum, so they all went home.
Then Dad made me some hot milk, helped me brush my teeth
and read me a bedtime story.

But there was no way
I was going to sleep,
not when there
were even BIGGER
plans to make!